SAFFRON'S WEDDING

WRITTEN AND ILLUSTRATED BY
JANEY JONES

Peppermint
press

Honeysuckle Cott
Cloppy's hom

Saffron Thimble's
Shop

Lavender
Lake

Lavender
Valley

Healing
Herb Garden

The Orchards

Aunt Marigold's
General Store

Bumblebees
Teashop

Wildsp
Woo

Summer
Meadow

Christmas
Corner

Honeypot Hill

Grandpa's House and Office

Honey-pot Cottage & The Blossom Bakehouse

Cornsilk Castle & The Courtyard

The Poppies

River Rushes (Honey and Mrs Bumble's home)

Peppermint Pond

Barley Farm

Sage's Vet Surgery

Rosehip School

Published by Peppermint Press, 10B Kings Haugh, Edinburgh

First published 2004

Design & Print by Century 23, 17-19 Maritime Lane, Edinburgh.

ISBN 0-9546170-1-0

Princess Poppy

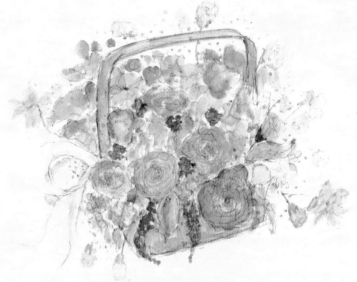

SAFFRON'S WEDDING

JANEY JONES

Peppermint
press

"Cornsilk Castle has never
looked so beautiful!"
said Poppy's Grandpa.

"Saffron's
wedding is going
to be the best
day of my life,"
declared Poppy.

"Honey and I are so
lucky to be bridesmaids,"
she said.

Poppy and Honey were helping Saffron to decorate the Great Hall of the Castle with flowers, satin ribbons and rose petals.

Grandpa was sitting on a throne-type chair, in the Great Hall, telling the girls what to do, without moving much himself!

Poppy looked out from a huge window
to the driveway below.
"Look at the cake! It's amazing!"
she exclaimed as the Wedding Cake was
carried from the double doors of a Blossom
Bakehouse van into the castle.

"See the flowers," gasped Honey, as the pink rosebuds were
carried from the Lavender Garden van.

Balloons arrived. Crystal glasses arrived. A violinist arrived.
Fresh strawberry cupcakes arrived. The photographer arrived.

Everyone in Honeypot Hill was busy with Saffron's marriage to
the vet, Mr. David Sage, of Barley Farm.

Suddenly, at the end of all the deliveries, Poppy's mummy arrived in a little green van with red writing, which said: *Saffron's Sewing Shop.*

"Oh, mummy's here with the dresses!" exclaimed Poppy.

Poppy and Honey ran down to see the dresses, with Grandpa following behind them.

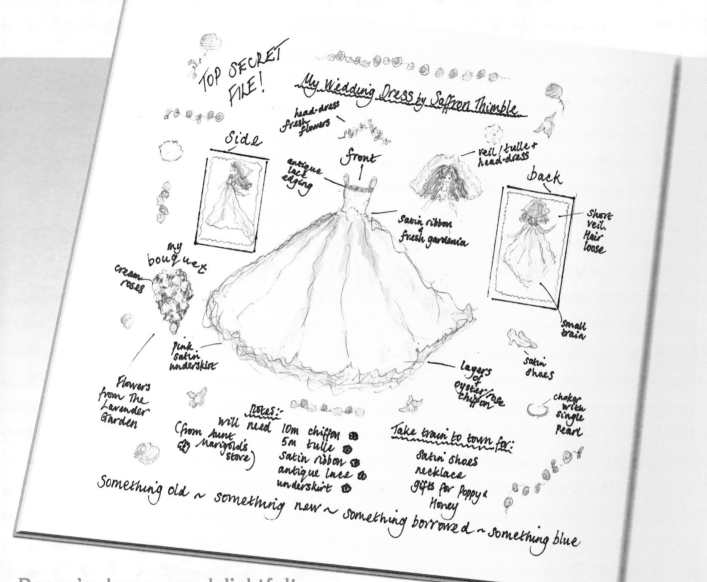

Poppy's dress was delightful!
Honey's dress was adorable!

But Saffron's dress was truly perfect-
just as she had imagined it....

Poppy and Honey went with
Grandpa to place the dresses
in the little dressing room
where they would get ready
later that day.

"Now girls," said Grandpa,
firmly,"whatever you do, don't
touch the dresses until
Saffron says so."

Grandpa went back to join Mummy in the Great Hall.

At first, Poppy and Honey followed Grandpa, but they couldn't help looking back at their chiffon dresses hanging so beautifully in the dressing room.

"I've got to try my dress on!" decided Poppy. "Let's go back," she whispered.

Honey agreed. They just had to see how they looked. So they tip-toed back to the dressing room and carefully began to step into their chiffon dresses.

Honey helped Poppy with the pink rosebud buttons.

Poppy helped Honey with the green satin sash.

They helped one another with their pink silk neck chokers. Then they both stepped into their little pink slippers.

"You are such a perfect princess, Poppy," Honey told her friend, as she handed her a posy of roses to hold.

"And you are such a delicate fairy, Honey," Poppy replied.

They held hands and danced around the dressing room.

Suddenly, Honey felt worried.
"What if someone sees us! Remember what your Grandpa said...
she recalled.

Reluctantly, the girls took off their dresses and hung them
back on the satin hangers.

Then Poppy had a thought. She looked at Honey.
Then she looked at Saffron's Wedding Dress.
Then she looked back at Honey.

"Poppy! You cannot try that one on. It's Saffron's
special dress," warned Honey.

"But she wouldn't mind," said Poppy confidently.
"In fact, if she was here, she would say: 'Poppy, certainly
you can try this on'," announced Poppy, grandly.

Honey closed her eyes as Poppy took the precious Wedding Dress off its hanger. Poppy stepped inside Saffron's magical silk gown.

It was much too big for Poppy, even though Saffron was a very dainty grown-up.

"I may as well put Saffron's shoes on too," she explained to Honey, "just to get the right look."

"I just need to look in a mirror, then I'll definitely take it off," she said. Then she walked across the dressing room, teetering in the high-heeled shoes and humming
"here comes the bride" as she went.

All of a sudden, Poppy lost her balance and fell over, catching the heel of Saffron's shoe in the delicate hem of the Wedding Dress.

"Rrrrip!"

Poppy collapsed in a crumpled heap.
"Ouch! Help!" she cried. "Oh No! I've torn Saffron's Wedding Dress," Poppy sobbed.
"I've ruined everything. What am I going to do?"

"Take it off, and hang it up again. Maybe no one will notice," suggested Honey, fearfully. At first Poppy thought this was a good idea.

"No," she sighed, "we do have to tell Saffron what I've done." "Yes, you're right, we will have to tell her," agreed Honey, nervously.

Saffron was singing to herself in the Great Hall. She was hanging garlands of cornflowers, honeysuckle and jasmine.

"Hi, Poppy. Hi, Honey," she sang as she saw the two girls appear.

"What do you think of the flowers in the Great Hall?" Saffron asked.

Both little girls began to cry.

"Don't you like them?" asked Saffron,
sounding surprised.
"Oh, it's not the flowers!"
explained Poppy. "It's your dress!"
"You don't like my dress?"
whispered Saffron.
"Yes. Yes, we do! It's just that, well,
erm, you see, I tried it on and now
I've ruined it," wailed Poppy,
wiping her wet face.
"Oh no! Let's go and have a look,"
"I'm sure it can't be *that* bad,"
Saffron said, sounding calmer than
she felt.

Grandpa came with them to inspect the damage,
tutting and muttering, "Dear, oh dear," as he went.

"What were you thinking of, Poppy, trying on
Saffron's dress?" Grandpa asked.

"I am very, very sorry, Saffron,"
said Poppy softly, looking down.

Saffron examined the dress carefully, then she looked at her watch.

"Girls, we have two hours," she began, "I will need my pink sewing box from my shop and some more chiffon from Aunt Marigold's General Store. Grandpa, can you help the girls to get me these things?"

"Of course, Saffron, anything," said Grandpa.

Saffron managed to fix the torn dress beautifully.
"Come on girls. Now it's time to get ready-with my say so, this time!" Saffron announced.

Poppy, Honey and Saffron sat looking into a big gold-framed mirror as the hairdresser curled, pinned, flicked and sprayed their hair.

Then Poppy's mummy dabbed their lips with rosebud lip cream. And finally, they sprayed Honeysuckle scent on their wrists.

They all turned up at the chapel looking perfect.
Everyone gasped as they saw the beautiful dresses and
posies of the summer flowers.
"Look at the flower girls! They're little princesses,"
said one lady.

Poppy felt happy inside again now that everything had been sorted out. She waved over to her Mummy and Daddy and then to Mrs Bumble, and then to Grandpa.
Grandpa smiled at her for the first time in over two hours. What a lovely smile that was!

After the ceremony, Saffron gave Poppy and Honey each a pink satin handbag, with a silver handle.

These were gifts for being such special princess flower girls.

Then the photographer took pictures of Saffron, with Poppy and Honey. Poppy smiled for the photographer. "Thank goodness everything has turned out alright!" she thought.

Later, at the party in the Great
Hall, Poppy said shyly to Grandpa,
"Grandpa, am I still a real princess?"

Grandpa paused.

"Yes Poppy, you are a very real princess. And you are a very
honest princess, and that is the best sort of princess to be."

Poppy and Grandpa danced together up and down the Great Hall.
"Saffron's wedding really has been the very best day of my life!"
decided Princess Poppy.

"WITH ALL MY LOVE TO MATTHEW, WHO
MAKES ALL MY DREAMS COME TRUE."

ALSO AVAILABLE :

Princess Poppy's Party
ISBN 0-95461-700-2

website : www.princesspoppy.com